Tadpoles
Fairytale Twists

The Ninjabread Man

Written by Katrina Charman

Illustrated by Fabiano Fiorin

Crabtree Publishing Company

www.crabtreebooks.com

Crabtree Publishing Company
www.crabtreebooks.com
1-800-387-7650

PMB 59051,
350 Fifth Ave., 59th Floor
New York, NY 10118

616 Welland Ave.
St. Catharines, ON
L2M 5V6

Published by Crabtree Publishing in 2016

Series editor: Melanie Palmer
Series designer: Peter Scoulding
Cover designer: Cathryn Gilbert
Series advisor: Catherine Glavina
Editor: Petrice Custance
Notes to adults: Reagan Miller
Prepress technician: Ken Wright
Print production coordinator: Margaret Amy Salter

Text © Katrina Charman 2015
Illustration © Fabiano Fiorin 2015

Printed in Canada/012016/BF20151123

First published in 2015 by Franklin Watts (A division of Hachette Children's Books)

Library and Archives Canada
Cataloguing in Publication

Charman, Katrina, author
     The ninjabread man / Katrina Charman ;
illustrated by Fabiano Fiorin.

(Tadpoles fairytale twists)
Issued in print and electronic formats.
ISBN 978-0-7787-2472-8 (bound).--
ISBN 978-0-7787-2568-8 (paperback).--
ISBN 978-1-4271-7724-7 (html)

     I. Fiorin, Fabiano, illustrator II. Title. III.
Series: Tadpoles. Fairytale twists

PZ7.1.C547Ni 2016   j823'.92   C2015-907117-8
                                       C2015-907118-6

Library of Congress
Cataloging-in-Publication Data

CIP available at Library of Congress

This story is based on the traditional fairy tale,
The Gingerbread Man, but with a new twist.
Can you make up your own twist for the story?

Once upon a time, in a small house in the forest, a lonely old man decided to make himself a friend. So he baked a gingerbread ninja—a Ninjabread man.

But when the Ninjabread man
turned golden brown, he jumped
up and ran out the door.

"Stop!" yelled the old man,
chasing after him.

But the Ninjabread man kept running, shouting: "Ka-Pow! Hi-Yah! And Shazam! You can't catch me, I'm the Ninjabread man."

Along the path, a hungry pig was sniffing for acorns beneath the mud. He saw the delicious Ninjabread man and shouted, "Stop, I want to eat you!"

10

The Ninjabread man twisted out of the way, singing: "Ka-Pow! Hi-Yah! And Shazam! You can't catch me, I'm the Ninjabread man."

At the edge of the forest, a herd of cows grazed in a field.

One of them spotted the yummy
Ninjabread man and squeezed
through the fence.
"Stop! I want to eat you!"
the cow cried.

14

The Ninjabread man rolled
right over the cow's back.
"Ka-Pow! Hi-Yah! And Shazam!
You can't catch me, I'm the
Ninjabread man."

Farther down the hill, a flock of chicks pecked at the ground looking for grain. One by one, they smelled the Ninjabread man as he whirled and twirled toward them.

"Stop! We want to eat you!"
They rushed toward him with their
hungry beaks open wide.

18

But the Ninjabread man
backflipped over them.
"Ka-Pow! Hi-Yah! And Shazam!
You can't catch me, I'm the
Ninjabread man," he chuckled.

Then he reached a deep, wide river.
He searched for a way to get
across without getting soggy.

A crafty fox was watching.
"I'll help you cross the river," he
said. "Just climb onto my back."

"STOP!" yelled the old man, who had finally caught up. "I can teach you to jump this river in one single bound."

The Ninjabread man laughed.
"Ha, ha! I don't need help from
anyone! I'm the Ninjabread man!"

He took a flying leap but missed
the bank, landing on a drooping
tree branch.

To his surprise, the old man leaped across the water, grabbing the Ninjabread man's arm and taking him safely to the other side.

"Wow!" gasped the Ninjabread man. "Can you teach me those moves?" The old man nodded.

Soon the Ninjabread man was the star of Ninja school. He learned how to jump across rivers—and avoid hungry foxes!

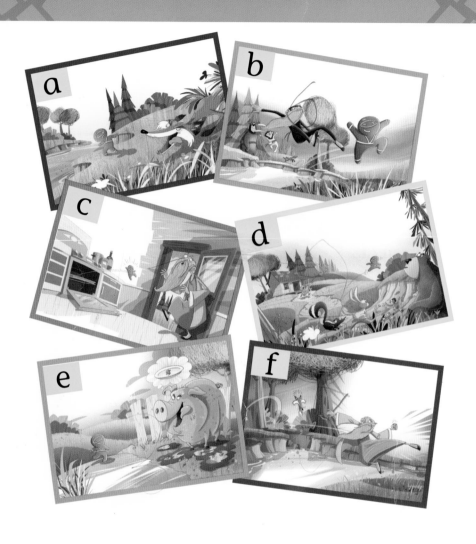

Put these pictures in the correct order. Which event do you think is the most important? Now try writing the story in your own words!

Puzzle 2

1. I can flip and jump!

2. I love baking cookies.

3. I have big jaws!

4. I don't always tell the truth.

5. I can teach Ninja!

6. I do not know how to swim!

Choose the correct speech bubbles for each character. Can you think of any others? Turn the page to find the answers for both puzzles.

Notes for Adults

TADPOLES: Fairytale Twists are engaging, imaginative stories designed for early fluent readers. The books may also be used for read-alouds or shared reading with young children.

TADPOLES: Fairytale Twists are humorous stories with a unique twist on traditional fairy tales. Each story can be compared to the original fairy tale, or appreciated on its own. Fairy tales are a key type of literary text found in the Common Core State Standards.

The following PROMPTS before, during, and after reading support literacy skill development and can enrich shared reading experiences:

1. **Before Reading:** Do a picture walk through the book, previewing the illustrations. Ask the reader to predict what will happen in the story. For example, ask the reader what he or she thinks the twist in the story will be.

2. **During Reading:** Encourage the reader to use context clues and illustrations to determine the meaning of unknown words or phrases.

3. **During Reading:** Have the reader stop midway through the book to revisit his or her predictions. Does the reader wish to change his or her predictions based on what they have read so far?

4. **During and After Reading:** Encourage the reader to make different connections:
   Text-to-Text: How is this story similar to/different from other stories you have read?
   Text-to-World: How are events in this story similar to/different from things that happen in the real world?
   Text-to-Self: Does a character or event in this story remind you of anything in your own life?

5. **After Reading:** Encourage the child to reread the story and to retell it using his or her own words. Invite the child to use the illustrations as a guide.

Here are other titles from TADPOLES: Fairytale Twists for you to enjoy:

Answers

Puzzle 1
The correct order is: 1c, 2d, 3e, 4a, 5f, 6b

Puzzle 2
The old man: 2, 5
The Ninjabread man: 1, 6
The fox: 3, 4